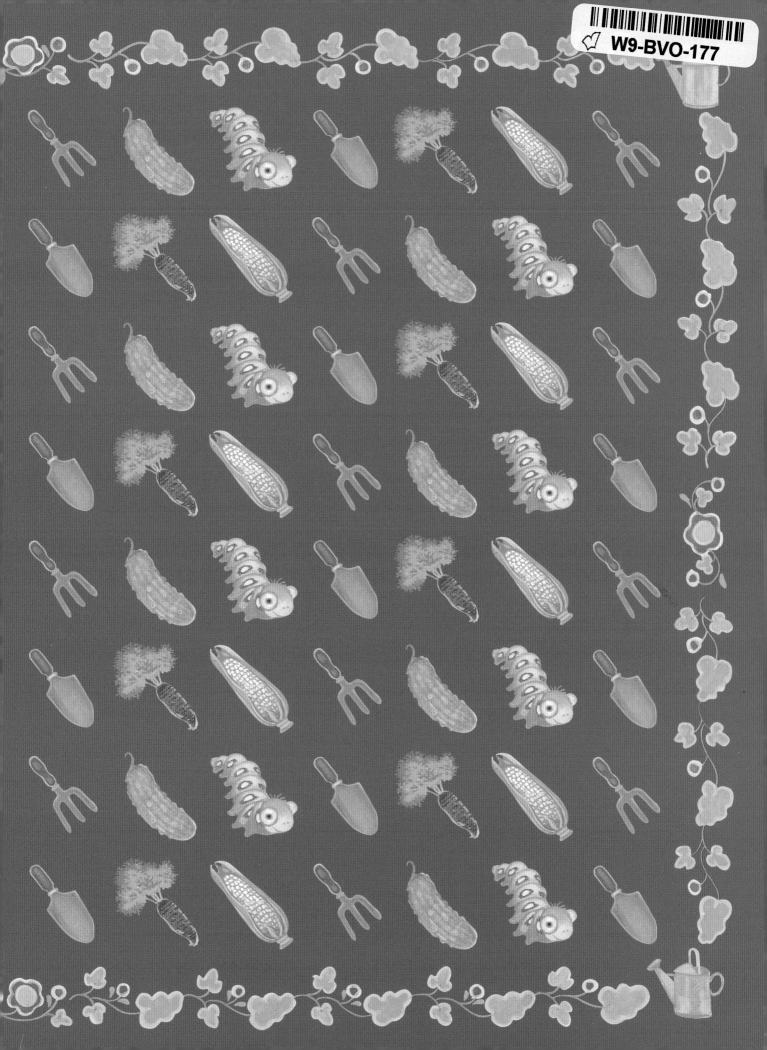

TINY GREEN THUMBS

C. Z. GUEST

ILLUSTRATED BY
LORETTA KRUPINSKI

HYPERION BOOKS FOR CHILDREN

NEW YORK

with thanks to katherine Tegen
for her help with the text

For information address Hyperion Books for Children,
114 Fifth Avenue, New York, New York 10011-5690.
Printed in Hong Kong by South China Printing Company, Ltd.
Book is set in 13 Pt. Bernhard Gothic and 12 Pt. Providence Sans.
The artwork for each picture was prepared using gouache and colored pencil.
Designed by Christine Kettner
First Edition
1 3 5 7 9 10 8 6 4 2

Library of Congress Cataloging-in-Publication Data
Guest, C.Z.
Tiny green thumbs / C.Z. Guest; illustrated by Loretta Krupinski.
p. cm.
Summary: Tiny Bun and his grandmother plan, plant, and grow a
vegetable garden. Includes step-by-step instructions for planting
carrots, beans, cucumbers, corn, and sunflowers.
ISBN 0-7868-0516-1 (tr.)
[1. Vegetable gardening—Fiction. 2. Gardening—Fiction. 3. Grandmothers—Fiction.
4. Rabbits—Fiction.] I. Krupinski, Loretta, ill. II. Title.
PZ7.G9374Ti 2000   [E]—dc21
99-41306   CIP

Visit www.hyperionchildrensbooks.com,
part of the GO Network

To Gregory, Winston, and Ivor
with love
—Ganny

TINY BUN wanted to grow a garden. Little Mouse wanted to help. But Tiny Bun wasn't sure how to go about doing it. There were a lot of tools in the garden shed that he wanted to use—a trowel, a fork, a hoe, and especially the hose. Up on a shelf he could see some packets of seeds. How could he make them grow?

His Ganny Bun was loving, wise, and very cool. "There are six things you need to grow a garden," she told Tiny Bun.

"What's the first thing?" he asked.

"Soil," Ganny Bun replied. "You first need to make a garden bed. I'll show you how to do that."

STARTING YOUR GARDEN

1. Pick a sunny spot close to the house or close to some place where you can get water for your garden.

2. Get a ball of string and four wooden sticks or stakes.

3. Put a stick in the ground and take 13 hops. Put another stick in the ground. Take the string and tie it to each stick. Make sure it's tight.

4. Take your shovel and dig a little trench under the string in a straight line. This is the first side of your bed.

5. Now square off your garden by doing the same thing for the remaining three sides.

"I have a nice square garden bed. Now what?" asked Tiny Bun.

"Now we have to get the soil ready. Let me help you—this is hard work," said Ganny.

GETTING THE SOIL READY

1. Take your garden fork and dig down three or four times.

2. Loosen up and turn over all the dirt until it's nice and light with no grass or rocks in it.

3. Take a bag of fertilizer, tear a small hole in the corner, and spread it back and forth over the garden bed.

4. Using your fork or hoe, mix the fertilizer thoroughly into the soil so that it is spread evenly throughout the garden bed.

5. Hook up your hose to the outdoor water spigot and water the soil very gently.

"The soil is ready. Now what?" asked Tiny Bun.

"The second thing you need is a seed. But you might want to plant more than one." Ganny Bun smiled.

"Ten seeds! Twenty seeds! Maybe even a hundred seeds.

"Well, let's see what we have here." Ganny Bun took five different kinds of seeds from the shelf in the shed.

Tiny Bun carefully tore off a corner of the carrot seed pack.
He poured three of the tiny seeds into his hand. "Now what?"
he asked.

"Let's plant them," said Ganny Bun. "I'll show you how."

PLANTING CARROTS

1. Take a stick and make a shallow trough in the dirt.

2. Carrot seeds are tiny, so tear off a corner of the packet, leaving a small hole big enough for only one or two seeds to fit through at a time.

3. Gently shake the seeds into the trough from one end of the row to the other. The tiny seeds should be spread evenly down the row.

4. Cover the seeds with dirt and smooth the dirt over the trough gently.

5. Pat down firmly and water lightly.

Tiny Bun couldn't stop hopping up and down.

He was so excited.

"Can we do another row now?"

PLANTING BEANS

1. Take two hops and a jump (about two feet) from your row of carrot seeds.

2. Make a trough a little deeper than the one you made for the carrots.

"Of course," said Ganny Bun. "How about the green beans next?"

3. Cut open the packet of seeds and sprinkle them into the trough.

4. Cover gently with dirt, pat down, and water.

"I think we should plant corn next," said Tiny Bun.

"A good idea," said Ganny Bun.

"Corn takes a lot of room to grow. We must plant at least four rows," said Ganny Bun. "I'll show you how. Here are two packets of sweet corn so we don't run out."

"May I hold a packet?" asked Tiny Bun.

PLANTING CORN

1. To plant four rows of corn, separate each row by three feet. Plant at least four rows side by side.

2. Take a stick and make a little trench about two inches deep.

3. Water the soil well before you plant. Lay your seeds one by one in your little trench two and a half to three inches apart. Do this all the way down the four rows.

4. Brush the dirt back into the trench, covering the seeds. Water gently.

"What about the cucumbers? I love cucumbers," said Tiny Bun.

"Cucumbers are a little different," said Ganny Bun. "Cucumber plants have crawling vines that need plenty of room to grow properly. And the more you pick them, the more cucumbers will grow on the vines. One plant can grow eight, or nine, or ten cucumbers!"

"Show me how, Ganny Bun."

PLANTING CUCUMBERS

1. In one corner of the garden, scoop up the dirt and make four cucumber mounds. The hills should be at least two feet from one another and about the size of home plate on a baseball field.

2. Plant four to six seeds three inches deep in each little hill.

3. Water well.

"There's one packet left, Ganny Bun. What are these flowers?" asked Tiny Bun.

"Those are sunflowers. They got their name because they turn their faces to the sun all day. They can grow very tall—ten feet tall—so we have to make sure that we don't plant them too close together."

PLANTING SUNFLOWERS

1. In the remaining corner of your garden make two short rows in the dirt. The rows need to be three feet apart.

2. Plant the seeds one foot apart and cover them with half an inch of soil.

3. Firm the soil and water gently.

"We planted all the seeds. Now what?" asked Tiny Bun.

"We have the soil and the seeds. We added water—that was the third thing. There are three more things that we need to make a garden. Guess what they are."

"I don't know," said Tiny Bun.

"What's up in the sky?" asked Ganny Bun.

"Birds," said Tiny Bun.

"Well, that's true, but birds won't help your garden grow. What else? What's shining in your eyes right now?"

"The sun!" said Tiny Bun.

"That's right. And all living things need the sun to grow properly."

"What else do they need?" asked Tiny Bun.

"They need time. Time to grow," said Ganny Bun.

"How much time?" asked Tiny Bun.

"At least a few weeks. Three or four weeks," said Ganny Bun.

"Four weeks! That's a long time. I can't wait that long.
What can I do for four weeks?"

"You can use your tiny green thumbs," said Ganny Bun.

"My thumbs aren't green, Ganny Bun."

"They will be if you use them well."

MAKING YOUR GARDEN GROW

1. Every day you need to check the garden. Water it lightly early in the morning, making sure that every plant has enough to drink.

2. In two weeks or less, you will see little seeds coming up through the soil.

3. Three weeks after planting, spray each plant and the soil around it with a liquid fertilizer, following the directions on the bottle. Spray lightly and thoroughly as if you were watering.

4. Keep your garden bed tidy by pulling out any pesky weeds. Remember where your rows are so you don't mistake your plants for weeds. You might want to put a little name tag on a stake by each row so you can remember what you've planted where.

"How long has it been since we planted the seeds now, Ganny Bun?" asked Tiny Bun.

"Four weeks."

"My thumbs aren't green—what's wrong?"

"Well, there might be some more things you need to do in your garden. Then your thumbs might turn green."

"Like what?" asked Tiny Bun.

"Let me show you."

CARING FOR YOUR GARDEN

1. If you find any bugs in your garden, pick them off.

2. Keep your plant leaves clean by gently wiping them with a wet sponge.

3. Don't forget your garden needs to be watered every day. If you do this right, by the end of July you'll be able to play hide-and-seek among the cornstalks.

One day, Tiny Bun was checking his garden. He was looking under the green vines that were growing like a creepy crawly blanket in the cucumber corner of the garden.

"Ganny Bun! There are little pickles under here," he called.

"Those are the cucumbers."

"And look! There are some green beans here," said Tiny Bun.

"They'll be ready to harvest soon."

"But Ganny, my thumbs aren't green yet."

"Are you sure? Let's look and see."

Tiny Bun looked closely at his thumbs. He had been watering his garden and pulling weeds. His paws were damp and there were dirt and bits of weeds stuck to them.

"My thumbs are pink and brown and green," said Tiny Bun.

"That's because you added the final thing that makes a garden grow," said Ganny Bun.

"What's that?"

"Love. And look at your garden now," said Ganny Bun.

The garden was filled with green flourishing vegetables and flowers.

"It's very green," said Tiny Bun.

"That means you have tiny green thumbs, Tiny Bun."

"It does?"

"Of course. Now, let's go harvest your garden and eat everything that you've grown."

And so they did.